THE MAGIC CUP AND SAUCER

JANE MARRINER

AuthorHouse™ UK
1663 Liberty Drive
Bloomington, IN 47403 USA
www.authorhouse.co.uk
UK TFN: 0800 0148641 (Toll Free inside the UK)
UK Local: 02036 956322 (+44 20 3695 6322 from outside the UK)

Because of the dynamic nature of the Internet, any web addresses or links contained in this book may have changed since publication and may no longer be valid. The views expressed in this work are solely those of the author and do not necessarily reflect the views of the publisher, and the publisher hereby disclaims any responsibility for them.

This book is printed on acid-free paper.

ISBN: 979-8-8230-8302-7 (sc)
ISBN: 979-8-8230-8303-4 (e)

Library of Congress Control Number: 2023910449

Print information available on the last page.

Published by AuthorHouse 07/12/2023

authorHOUSE

THE
MAGIC CUP
AND
SAUCER

An enormous cup and saucer floated down from the sky, and settled in a field alongside the river. It was home to three firm friends.

There was Caterina Cat who wore a hat with a long trailing feather.

Doggie Dog sported a large bow-tie, and Toddle Tortoise proudly carried a red shell on his back.

Their cup and saucer was a magic cup and saucer and could sail through the air, around the globe to wherever the three friends chose.

It used no fuel of any kind for travelling, and so did not fill the skies with harmful gases or dirty fumes.

When it rained, the three friends placed the saucer above the cup to keep themselves cosy and dry.

Now, Caterina Cat, Doggie Dog and Toddle Tortoise climbed out of their home to visit Mister Horatio Honeycomb. He looked after the apple orchard next to the field, and they found him tending to his beehive.

There were pretty spring blossoms on the orchard trees. The bees were getting ready to spread their pollen from flower to flower, to help the trees to produce seed for growing into Autumn apples.

Mister Horatio Honeycomb eagerly listened to the friends' latest adventure.

"Our magic cup and saucer took us to the African plains" said Caterina Cat.

"Temperatures are rising and it was very hot, with no rain to fill all the water holes."

"A zebra, a giraffe and a buffalo climbed into our magic cup and saucer. We skimmed over the land until we found a large full water hole where they enjoyed drinking, bathing and gossiping with other African animals", explained Doggie Dog.

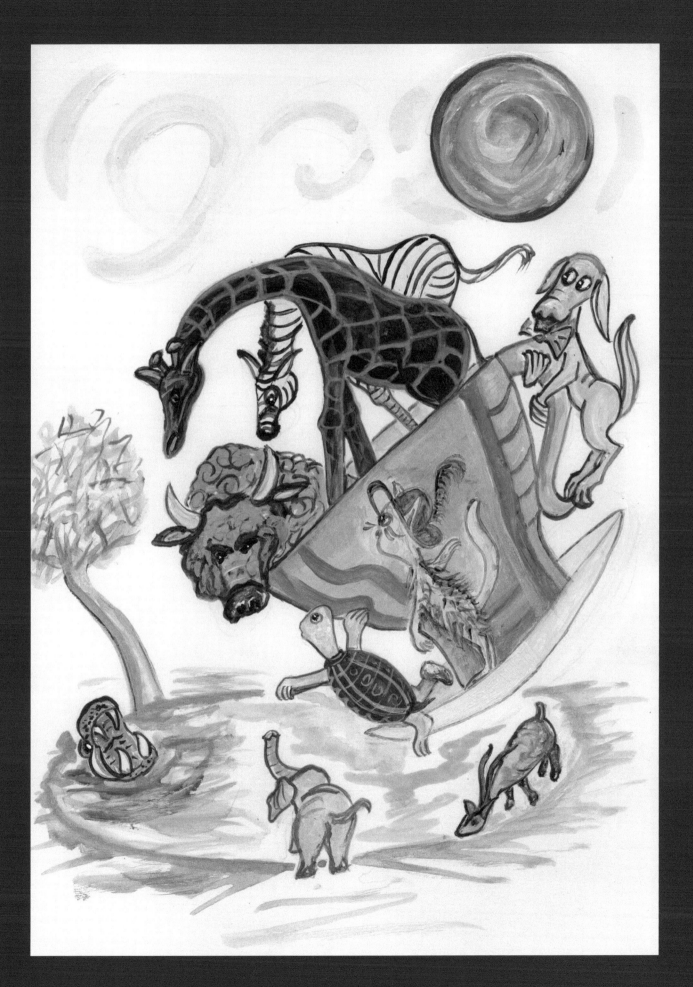

"Then, as we recrossed the African plain, we spied a lonely baby elephant down below" said Toddle Tortoise. "We landed our magic cup and saucer nearby to talk to him. He told us that his elephant family had moved off in search for plants to eat and another water hole."

"I don't know what to do, as I am too small to keep up with them" sighed the baby elephant, sadly.

The three friends coaxed the baby elephant into their magic cup and saucer. Shortly afterwards, they found an elephant sanctuary where the baby elephant could eat and drink as much as he could manage, and there were other baby elephants for him to talk and play with.

"Then, we bid farewell to Africa, and here we are home again!" finished Doggie Dog.

Caterina Cat, Doggie Dog and Toddle Tortoise went back to their magic cup and saucer home, to eat a late supper and retire to bed.

That night, there was a terrible storm with torrential rain and violent winds. In the morning, the river was swollen with the heavy rain, and there was a desperate buzzing noise on the side of the magic cup and saucer. It was Polonius Honeybee.

"Please help", he buzzed. "The storm has swept the beehive into the river, and water is seeping into the beehive. I am the only honeybee with dry wings! How are we going to pollinate the apple blossom now if none of us can fly?"

"We are coming" assured the three friends, "but we cannot swim" wailed Caterina Cat and Toddle Tortoise. However, Doggie Dog could swim very well. So he left his bow-tie on the river bank for safety, and paddled out to the floating beehive.

Mister Horatio Honeycomb was jumping up and down in despair, but managed to throw a log across the river to Doggie Dog. Doggie Dog placed the log against the beehive and slowly used the log to push the beehive to the river bank where the magic cup and saucer were ready and waiting.

Caterina Cat and Toddle Tortoise heaved the lid off the beehive.

"Now, Toddle Tortoise, put my hat on your head. You need to stretch yourself between the magic cup and saucer and the top of the beehive," commanded Caterina Cat.

Polonius Honeybee told the bees to form a long queue.

"Carefully make your way, one at a time, across the feathered hat, along Toddle Tortoise's shell, and then drop into the magic cup and saucer" informed Polonius Honeybee.

There were a great many very wet bees, and their leader, Queen Bee was reluctant to leave her precious beehive, so it took all day to empty the beehive and to shelter the bees in the magic cup and saucer.

"There is an old tree with a huge hole in its tree trunk at the far end of the orchard", Mister Horatio Honeycomb told Queen Bee. "Your honey bees will be safe in there, and their wings will soon dry out. I will set up a new beehive for them, and they will soon be flying happily amongst the apple blossoms again."

The magic cup and saucer carried the bees to the old tree, and Polonius Honeybee helped the bees to climb out of the magic cup and saucer and to crawl up the tree trunk to their new home down the large hole. Queen Bee was the last to enter, having first seen her honeybee colony snugly inside.

Afterwards, Queen Bee and Polonius Honeybee thanked Mister Horatio Honeycomb, Caterina Cat, Doggie Dog and Toddle Tortoise for all their help.

The water in the river ebbed to its normal level, and the sun shone once again.

Autumn came, and Mister Horatio Honeycomb celebrated a wonderful apple harvest. He invited Caterina Cat, Doggie Dog, and Toddle Tortoise to honey tarts and apple crumble with ice cream. Everyone agreed it was the best meal they had ever eaten!

Printed in the United States
by Baker & Taylor Publisher Services